CAROUSEL

Brian Wildsmith

ALFRED A. KNOPF ~ NEW YORK

The fair was coming at last. Every year it visited the little town where Rosie and her brother Tom lived.

All the children ran out of the town to watch for the trucks that carried the fair.

As dusk fell, the fair drove into town. The children cheered
with joy.

When they went to bed that night, they were so excited they
could hardly sleep.

The next day Rosie and Tom watched workers set up the fair.

When all was ready, they raced to the carousel. That was the ride they loved best.

Around and around they went. "I wish I could ride the carousel forever!" shouted Rosie.

But after a few days the fair moved on to another town. The children were sad to see it go. "Don't forget to come back next year," called Rosie.

That winter Rosie became ill, and the doctor was called.

He examined Rosie carefully and said that she would have to stay in bed until her fever was gone.

Spring came, but Rosie was still sick, and she was very sad. "You will get well," the doctor told her, "but it will take time." To her parents he said, "You must cheer Rosie up and give her hope."

Tom overheard what the doctor said and had an idea.

He went to find Rosie's friends. "We must cheer Rosie up,"
Tom said, "and give her hope." Then they all threw a coin in the
fountain and made a wish.

Tom went home and emptied his piggy bank. Then he went to
the toy shop.

The next afternoon Rosie's friends came to see her. Each friend had made a picture for Rosie.

"Cheer up, Rosie," they all said. "Please get well soon." And they unrolled their pictures.

"Oh, what beautiful paintings," said Rosie. "All my favorite things to ride on the carousel!" And there were the snowflake, the wings of time, the kangaroo…

the story chair, the unicorn, and the throne. "How I wish I could ride on them all right now!"

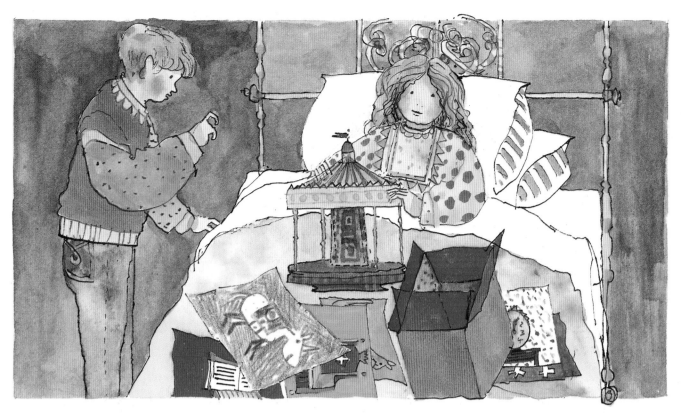

Then Tom gave Rosie his present. It was a little carousel that went around and around and played a pretty tune.

That night Rosie ran a high temperature. If only the carousel would come back, she thought as she was falling asleep.

As her eyes closed, Rosie heard a voice.
It came from the little carousel:

"Step aboard and we will fly
through the window, through the sky.

"Let me swing you to and fro
in a land of ice and snow."

With snowflakes falling everywhere,
her fever fell in the cold night air.

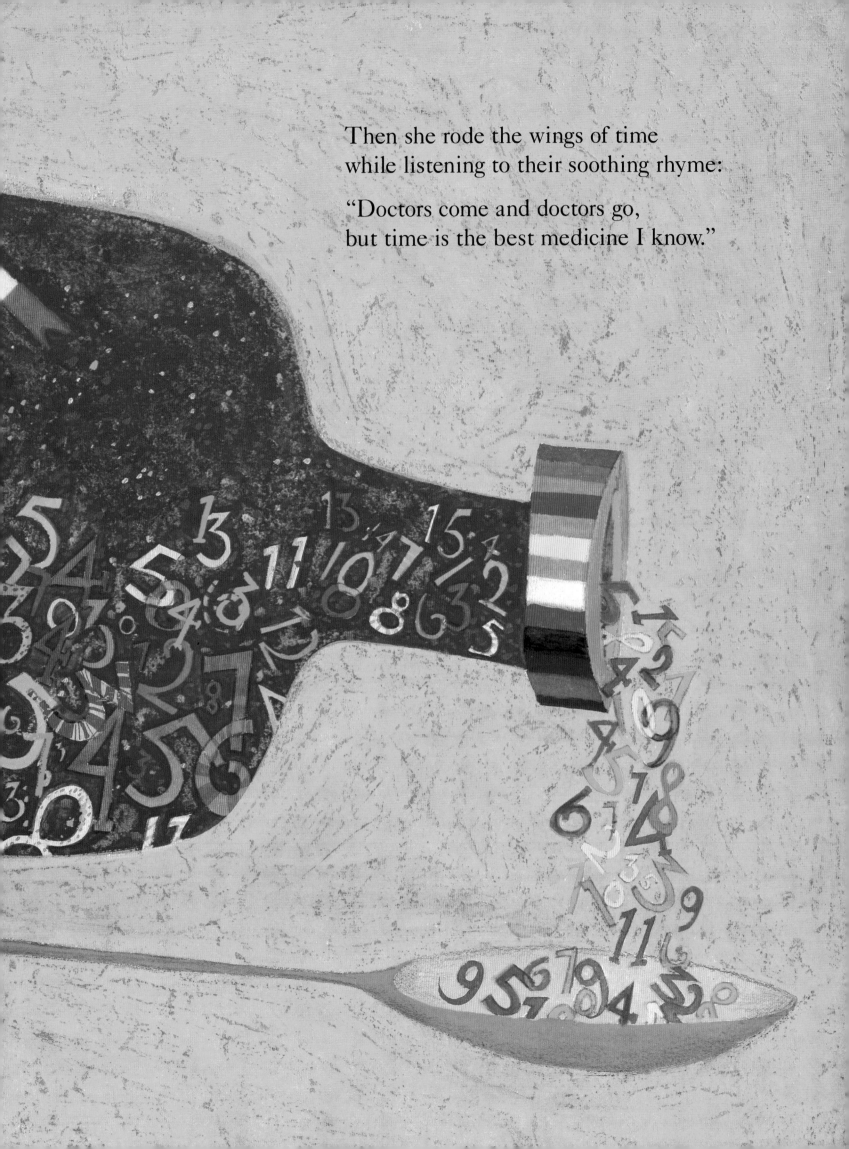

Then she rode the wings of time
while listening to their soothing rhyme:

"Doctors come and doctors go,
but time is the best medicine I know."

On she went, up through the air,
riding on the story chair,
to meet the friends
from books she'd read
each day as she lay sick in bed.

Then safe aboard the kangaroo
through the moonlit night she flew.

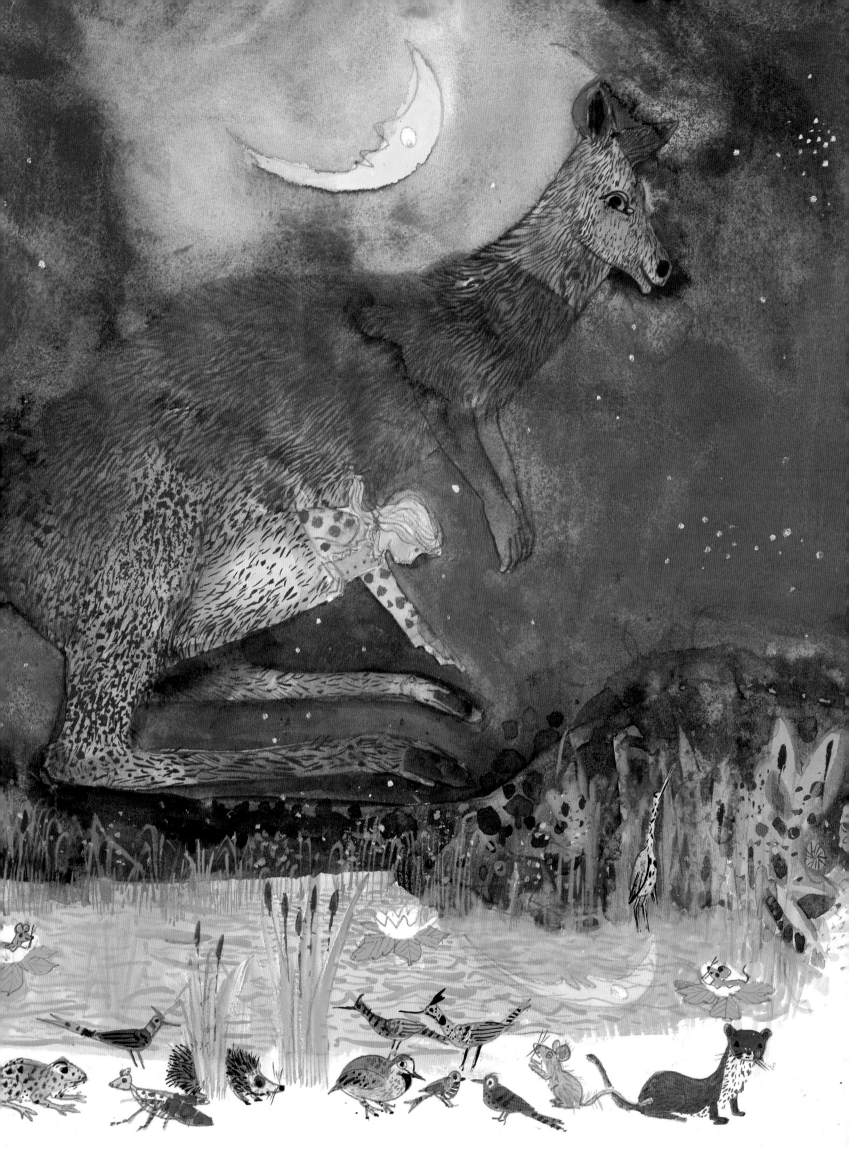

In splendor she was carried high
on a throne into the sky,
toward the moon all shining bright
on that magic, starry night.

And galloping through the Milky Way
she rode on freely toward the day.

Bump! Rosie awoke, sprawled on the floor beside her bed.

That morning the doctor came to see her. "Good heavens, Rosie, you look so much better!" he said.

As the days passed, Rosie got stronger and stronger. The doctor came for the last time and told her she was completely well and could go out to play.

Tom rushed out to tell Rosie's friends. And as they waited by Rosie's house to welcome her, the fair came back to town.

Rosie and her friends
watched the fair go up.
Then they raced to the
carousel. Rosie rode on
everything. "Thank you,
carousel, thank you," she
said as she went around
and around.

This time when the fair left town Rosie
was not sad, for she knew it was the carousel
that had given her hope.

For Joy, who was so brave

THIS IS A BORZOI BOOK PUBLISHED BY ALFRED A. KNOPF, INC.

Copyright © 1988 by Brian Wildsmith
All rights reserved under International and Pan-American Copyright
Conventions. Published in the United States by Alfred A. Knopf, Inc.,
New York. Distributed by Random House, Inc., New York.
First published in Great Britain by Oxford University Press in 1988.
Manufactured in Hong Kong 10 9 8 7 6 5 4 3 2 1
Library of Congress Cataloging-in-Publication Data
Wildsmith, Brian. Carousel.
Summary: While she is sick in bed,
a little girl dreams of riding on her favorite merry-go-round.
[1. Merry-go-round—Fiction. 2. Dreams—Fiction.
3. Sick—Fiction] I. Title. PZ7.W647Car 1988 [E] 88-846
ISBN 0-394-81937-3   ISBN 0-394-91937-8 (lib. bdg.)